MOUSSE AND MAYHEM

A BELLE HARBOR COZY MYSTERY (BOOK 11)

SUE HOLLOWELL

Mousse and Mayhem

Copyright © 2022 by Sue Hollowell

All rights reserved.

Cover design by Donna L. Rogers dlrcoverdesigns.com

Editing by: Tiffany White at Writers Untapped

CONTENTS

CHAPTER ONE

The front door of the bakery swung open as my bestie Fiona breezed inside. The initial rush of customers who had retrieved their early morning coffee and treats had dissipated. I wiped down tables and straightened the white wrought-iron chairs, readying the space for the next crowd. People came in waves as the day progressed, supplying themselves for their beach activities.

"Hey there," Fiona greeted, coming to give me a squeeze. She bounded in, her long blonde ponytail swinging behind her. Today was the day she officially began the renovations on her bar. The expansion was long overdue, as she was packed wall-to-wall most every day and night. Our weekend in Diamond Hills to research possibilities had given her a vision. Extending her dining room with outdoor seating to the front and side of her bar would almost double its capacity.

I tucked the towel into my apron pocket and held my arms out wide. I was incredibly blessed since my move to Belle Harbor with the most loving people surrounding me. A bestie, a quirky but fiercely protective uncle, and a boyfriend who supported me with all of my wacky ways. And to top it off, owning a thriving bakery in the legacy of my one-of-a-kind grandma Luna. I regularly pinched myself to believe it was all real, worlds away from my former life.

"Can you load me up an order of all the regulars for my crew?" Fiona asked, sweeping her arm toward the display case.

"You got it," I said. I retrieved a box from the back counter and gathered several varieties of our pastries for her to-go package.

"Maybe I should make it a double batch for the construction team as well," she added.

I closed the lid on box number one and retrieved a second. "How's that going?" I asked. Fiona had taken out a pretty large loan to cover the cost of adding to her bar. A common business practice, but she was betting she could expand her customer base enough to cover the payments. Extending myself that much financially gave me hives. I knew I could make a similar expansion successful, but going that far into debt was too much for me at the moment.

"Can you get away for a quick peek?" she asked. "The plans are set, and I can't wait. I only hope it goes quickly to minimize disruption for current customers."

I handed Fiona both boxes and rang up the purchase. She fished her credit card out and handed it to me. I peered over her shoulder, not seeing anyone else headed into the bakery. Holding up a finger toward Fiona, I ducked my head through the door into the kitchen. My assistant Linda was almost done with the second batch of baking for the day. Now would be a good time for a quick break to speed down to Fiona's and check out the plans.

I removed my apron, tucking it onto the shelf under the cash register. "I can come for a super short visit. I'm so excited to see what this is going to look like," I said. I held the door for Fiona, and we exited onto the boardwalk for the short distance to her bar at the end of the row of beachfront shops.

"I'm surprised you have any time on your hands with the wedding planning," Fiona said.

Chuckling, I said, "I would go without sleep to make it the perfect wedding for Unkie and Linda." Serendipitously, Uncle Jack had agreed to run an estate sale for Linda, something he normally didn't do. His Checkered Past Antiques shop kept him more than occupied, but a spark ignited between the two of them, and the flame has fanned hot ever since. Luckily for me, Linda was also an excellent baker and accepted my offer to join team Luna. Nobody was happier for Unkie than I was to finally see him receiving the happiness he deserved. His generosity to others in the community was legendary, and taking me in when I arrived on his doorstep . . . Well, I was beyond grateful.

"It's going to be epic, as it should be," Fiona said.

As we passed Mocha Joe's Coffee Shop, I peered inside at the throng of customers, the lobby constantly full to receive their caffeine fix. My first business collaboration way back when I started now flourished with Joe, one of my biggest wholesale customers. He had shared with me on my early morning delivery the prolific burglar had finally hit his place. To date, my bakery had been spared, but if this person wasn't caught, I believed it was only a matter of time. Thankfully, nobody was hurt in the thievery, and I hoped it stayed that way. They dedicated the town council agenda for their next meeting to business owners and how to stop the criminal.

"Any ideas on the culprit of these burglaries?" I asked. Fiona and I had paired up for multiple sleuthing sessions, her leading the way many times for our crime investigation.

The beach was sparsely populated as the sun had yet to burn off the low-lying fog hugging the shore. Ahead of us, beyond the boardwalk, the lighthouse poked out, a beacon for mariners. The predictable weather of Belle Harbor would certainly draw sizable crowds as the day wore on.

"A few things. But I don't know how helpful they are," she said.

"We need a bestie session at my place. Somehow, this person has to get caught before they do any more harm," I said.

"Agreed. What I know is that they seem to take small stuff and just enough to carry. I can't see a pattern in what they've nabbed. And it's during a time when most people are asleep," Fiona said.

"That window is pretty small," I said. Fiona's bar stayed open late and my bakery and Joe's opened very early. How was it that someone had not caught them yet? "Well, Unkie and I will be at the council meeting. I'll let you know if I learn anything."

We neared the end of the boardwalk and stopped just short of Fiona's. Pointing along the front of her bar and around the corner, she briefly described her vision of the outdoor area. Covered seating with strings of lights. Just enough to see in the dark but also provide a lovely ambiance. Her business would explode with this addition.

"Do you want to come in for a sec?" Fiona asked. "I can show you the architecture drawings." She grinned widely like a kid who just got the best present in the world. How could I say no?

"Quickly. I can't really leave Linda alone for long before the next rush," I said.

I pushed the door open to the quiet of the room. Fiona stepped inside and looked around, brows furrowed. It appeared we were alone. Belle Harbor was safe enough to leave the door unlocked and the place unattended for a short amount of time. But not lately.

"Well, that's weird," Fiona said, gazing throughout the bar like she expected someone to jump out and yell surprise. After setting the boxes on a booth table, she walked behind the bar toward the back storage room.

I moved to the next booth where the architecture drawings sat for her expansion, and I flipped through the pages, marveling at how her dream was coming to life. I whipped my head around toward the blood-curdling scream coming from the direction of the room where Fiona had disappeared.

CHAPTER TWO

Jogging toward Fiona, my mind raced with plausible reasons for the scream. Did an accident happen? Was she hurt?

"Tilly!"

"Coming," I said, rounding the corner to the room with all of her supplies and bumping into her.

Spinning around, Fiona stood inches from me and said, "She's dead."

I peered over her shoulder and spotted the health department inspector splayed on the floor, frozen ravioli spilling out of a bag near her head. Looking up and down the hallway, searching for anyone else in the bar, I shook my head. It appeared someone had conked her with the hard little cheese-filled square pasta. But who and why?

"Fiona," I whispered and grabbed her hand, leading her from the room. "We have to call Barney."

She nodded and sniffled. Who wouldn't be upset with the death of another human, especially in your place of business? I also knew there was no love lost between Fiona and Holly Pickett. The inspector regularly wrote Fiona up for very minor infractions, every one of which Fiona appealed and prevailed. I couldn't imagine why Holly seemed to have it in for Fiona, except for jealousy. My bakery had escaped all violations so far, but it did not lull me into thinking it couldn't happen. I lead Fiona from the room, and she craned her neck back to observe the scene.

"Let's go sit for a minute and catch our breath," I said, still pondering why there wasn't anyone else in the bar. We chose a vacant booth and each took a seat, the loud squeak of the faux leather filling the room. "Fiona, where's Stacy?" I asked. Her long-time server normally opened the bar, prepping everything for the day. She slowly swiveled her head and shrugged.

"Fiona, somebody did this."

Perking up, she replied, "Not Stacy. She texted me she had an emergency with childcare and had to leave for a bit. She was leaving the door unlocked for delivery." Heading to the bar and returning with a tissue, she continued, "It's never been a problem before. And I didn't expect Holly until later today."

I dug my phone from my pocket and swiped to the messaging app. A pit quickly formed in my gut, and I was anxious about what this might mean for my friend. With my head bowed, I peeked at Fiona, who fidgeted with the tissue. Quickly I tapped out a message to Barney, vague but with enough detail to get him to her ASAP. Pressing send, I adjusted the phone volume to vibrate and placed it upside down on the table.

Looking around at the empty bar, I tried to imagine the sequence of events that led to Holly dead in the storage room with the ravioli sprawled over the floor. If this weren't so serious, I would laugh at how that sounded like an answer to one of my favorite games as a kid, Clue.

"Fiona, we'll figure this out," I said. Linda was going to have to hold the fort down at the bakery for a bit longer. I sent her and Unkie a joint text that I had been delayed on a delivery and would be there when I could. Wracking my brain for any questions before the official investigation began, I asked, "Can you tell if the delivery person has been here yet?" Belle Harbor was small enough that most everyone knew each other. The restaurant supply company did business here and in the surrounding geographic area, but Paul was still a local. A very congenial guy, always with a joke. He was such a people person and loved his job, where he could interact with so many during his deliveries.

Fiona raised her right shoulder in a half-hearted shrug. "I think so."

Should I make a quick jaunt back to the room to confirm before Barney arrived? As if on cue, the door swung open, letting in a small breeze to sweep out the heaviness of the situation.

Barney approached our table like he was ready to take our order. "Tilly?" he asked, looking back and forth between us. My message to him was to get here right away. He knew I didn't cry wolf, and this was serious.

Sliding out of the booth, I put my hand on Fiona's. "You probably need to come too," I said. I had never seen my always exuberant friend so mellow. And not in a relaxed way. She clenched her fists and inhaled deeply.

We silently filed down the hallway, stopping just short of the storage room door. I stepped around Fiona to the front and faced Barney, preparing him before we entered. "Fiona and I came back from the bakery and found Holly Pickett in here." There. Pandora's box was wide open.

"OK," Barney said and shifted to the front of the line into the doorway.

I squeezed past him just inside the door, gazing at the shelves. Indeed, to answer my earlier question, the delivery guy had been here. Not that I wanted sweet Paul to be the murderer, but having another person on the list gave me a glimmer of hope.

Moving along the wall like he was avoiding hot lava in the middle of the room, Barney had his phone out, snapping a few pics. The once frozen ravioli has softened into tan little goo squares, looking anything but edible. "Do you know why the ravioli is out like this?" he asked.

"They were frozen, and I think someone used the bag to hit Holly," I said. That seemed the only logical explanation.

"Fiona," Barney said, waiting for her acknowledgment.

Staring at Holly without blinking, she muttered, "Huh?"

Guiding us from the room into the hallway, Barney continued, "Do you know anyone who would do this?" I was sure he was hoping to get a long list of names for diverting any guilt away from her. Sadly, she shook her head. Barney took several more steps, typing into his phone, likely to get the crime scene techs here. Fiona's bar would be closed for business.

"Fiona!" Stacy jogged down the hall, holding out her hand. "I am so sorry." She furrowed her brows and lifted her arm in Barney's direction. "What's going on?"

"Holly is in the back room," I said. "She's dead."

Stacy slapped her hand over her mouth, eyes bulging with tears. "Fiona," she started, reaching for her boss.

Standing with her arms at her side, Fiona allowed Stacy to hug her.

Now was as good of a time as any to break it to her. "Stacy, she was murdered," I said.

"No," Stacy squeaked. "Who could have done it?"

"That's what I want to know," Barney said, joining our trio. "Fiona, I'm going to need a list of everyone with access to your place."

"OK," she replied.

"Maybe if I had been here . . ." Stacy started.

"You might have been in danger too," Fiona said, plopping down into a booth seat. She looked around. "Where's Ronnie?"

"He's always late," Stacy replied. "And Christina should be here any minute too. Oh, why did I leave?" Stacy moaned.

Barney slid into the seat across from Fiona, his notebook out. "I'm sorry, but I have to do this."

Joining Fiona on her side, I draped my arm around her shoulders as she nodded.

"You and Holly were always arguing," Stacy blurted. Was she trying to escape the blame for this? And why immediately throw her loyal boss under the bus?

I hugged Fiona as she admitted her ongoing conflicts with Holly. Circumstances had escalated between them to the point Holly was paying unplanned visits to catch Fiona off guard and write her up with infractions. However, every single one had been appealed and overturned in Fiona's favor, further angering Holly.

"Fiona, I'll need you to come to the station for further questioning," Barney said, tucking his notebook into his inner pocket. That must have pained him to say that to someone who was like a daughter to him.

Her head popped up. "Am I a suspect?"

"I'm sure Barney is just being thorough. It sounds like there are a lot of people to talk to," I said. There was no way Fiona was involved in this. Was there?

CHAPTER THREE

Coins clanged into plastic buckets, echoing as we entered the Roseville Casino and Bar. Fiona needed a getaway from the stress of the investigation, and she suggested this venue in the neighboring town. Never visiting a casino in person, I only knew what I had seen on TV shows. She looped her arm around my elbow, leading me to a table with a dealer. Standing behind a chair, she pointed. "How about some blackjack?"

"Fiona," I started. "I have no idea how to play and I'll probably lose a ton of money."

The guy dealing cards didn't look old enough to legally be allowed in here. I glanced down at the row of similar tables and back toward several other games with blinking lights and ringing bells. Maybe I should just get a bucket of pennies and sit at a slot machine.

"Twenty-dollar minimum," the dealer said, not lifting his head and continuing to hand out cards to the three people seated in front of us. His name tag said Benji T.

Tugging Fiona's arm, I tipped my head toward the other side of the room, hoping for something that wouldn't cause me to mortgage my future.

"It's fine, Tilly," she said, pulling out a chair as the dealer wrapped up the previous hand. She fished in her purse and retrieved several bills, placing them on the table. The dealer shoved a stack of chips into the space in front of her.

I looked around, expecting to see guys in black suits with dark glasses and earpieces whispering into lapel mics. Pretty sure I had watched too many mob movies.

"Oh, hi Holly. Didn't recognize you when you first sat down," Benji said. He raised his arm and, using his pointer finger, gestured for someone to come to the table. "Let me get you your usual."

"I'm not Holly," Fiona muttered.

"Wow, so sorry about that," Benji said. "You look just like her." Shaking his head, he continued, "You two could definitely be sisters. Maybe she'll be here soon and you can see for yourself."

Fiona turned to me and frowned. Coming here had been to forget the drama back home in Belle Harbor. But the memory of Holly dead in her bar had been plopped right in front of Fiona.

As the server approached the table, Benji said, "False alarm. I thought this was one of our regulars," gesturing with cards in his hand toward Fiona.

"What can I get you, hon?" the server asked.

"Gin and tonic," Fiona replied as she shoved several chips toward the dealer, lifting the corner of the cards up for a peek.

Benji looked all around, inquiring whether any player wanted another card to add to their hand. Fiona waved her hand in a "come here" move to signal her request for another card. Benji turned a card faceup in front of Fiona.

She firmly put her hand down on the table, shoving her cards toward Benji, saying, "I surrender."

Finishing the hand with the remaining players, Benji scooped Fiona's chips toward him and slid chips toward another player who had won that round.

Setting her drink to Fiona's left, the server asked around the table for additional orders. Fiona took a yellow chip and handed it to the server. If my math was correct, that was a twenty-five-dollar tip. My pulse raced as I calculated how much Fiona had lost that round and how much value in chips sat in front of her. My stomach churned and gurgled as I worried about her irrational decision making. Was she being reckless in her fragile state of mind because of the murder? I couldn't blame her, but I also didn't want her to regret her rash decisions.

"Hey Fiona," came a deep voice from behind us. "Glad to see you again." A darker-skinned man with black hair appeared at the end of the table, his nametag announcing Keola—manager.

If the manager knew her by name, how often did she come here? My radar now buzzed hard with concern. Spending at the rate she was could very well make a dent in her budget for expanding the bar. Her vision was now in jeopardy.

Fiona smiled warmly at Keola. "Thank you."

"Dinner's on us. Enjoy!" he said, patting her gently on the back.

Getting comped dinner showed not only was she a regular, but that she spent enough that they wanted her to keep coming back. I had to get her away from this table before she was in too deep.

The dealer handed out cards all around. Fiona lifted the corner of hers up and shoved several different colored chips toward Benji. He glanced up at her as if to confirm she intended to go in that big. She nodded. Finished handing out cards to those who wanted them, Benji wrapped up the hand. Fiona turned her cards over and raised her arms in victory. She had twenty-one. Clapping like a giddy little girl, she continued to repeat the process, winning almost every hand.

Unable to take any more stress, I stepped forward and said, "Fiona, how about a break for dinner?"

She looked down at her mound of winnings, pondering. "I've got a hot hand, Tilly. A couple more, then you're on. I'm sorry. This probably isn't much fun for you," she said.

"OK." There was no deterring her. At least I suspected her mind was off the murder. How could it not be? I'd seen Fiona make some risky decisions before, usually fairly calculated, though. Tonight was extreme, even for her. I looked around the room, scouting out any other games that might be inclined to take less of her money. If I could only get her to quit while she was ahead, and then maybe play something a lot less pricey. But she seemed high on adrenaline. My only hope was dinner and drinks to bring her cortisol levels back in line.

That was going to be a tall order. The next two rounds she played doubled the size of the chip pile in front of her. She slid out of her chair as Benji traded her lower value chips for higher ones. From a hidden place, Fiona withdrew a bag I hadn't seen her carry in and loaded the remaining chips into it, sliding a few over to Benji for a tip.

"Thank you," he replied. "See you after dinner."

Not if I have anything to say about it, Benji. I draped my arm over Fiona's shoulder and headed toward the restaurant, the muscles in my stomach clenched so tight I struggled to breathe.

"Tilly, this trip has been just what the doctor ordered. I can't tell you how much better I feel." She quickened her pace.

That part of my mission was accomplished, but at what cost? I allowed my breath to slowly expand my ribs, daring not to say anything that would pick a fight with Fiona. If I could keep her from going into debt, I would call that a win.

The hostess recognized Fiona and led us to a booth along the wall. Fiddling with the menu, I pondered how much to quiz her about familiarity with this place. "What's good?" I asked, hoping my benign conversation could get us to a neutral spot.

"I try to have something I can't get in Belle Harbor. The orange chicken is my favorite," she said.

We slid our menus to the end of our table and waited on the return of the server to place our orders.

"Fiona, I have to ask," I started.

CHAPTER FOUR

Holding up her hand, Fiona said, "I know what you're going to say."

She probably did, but I felt like I had to say my piece. But how to broach it with care? The server appeared and grabbed our menus, taking our food and drink order. I let her get out of earshot before I leaned in and said, "I'm just a little surprised, that's all." That was putting it mildly. I knew Fiona was adventurous, but this bordered on risky behavior.

"I thought you might be," she replied, intertwining her fingers with her head bowed. "But you shouldn't worry. I'm actually pretty good. And when I lose, I limit myself."

I didn't know how you could do that. The hype of the game and the lure of just one more hand to win back what you lost would be incredibly tempting. The pile of chips Fiona left the table with was significantly smaller than when she started. If we left after dinner, she could at least limit any prospective losses.

"Aren't you worried about not having enough money for your renovation?" I asked. Maybe tying her behavior to something she dearly held might snap her out of it.

"Nah," she said, waving her hand. "I've done this long enough that I have a gut feeling." She took the drink from the server before it could hit the table, sucking half of it down.

I needed to trust her. Pushing any further would get me into dicey territory with our friendship, and I wasn't willing to chance it. But you better believe I would watch her like a hawk. And maybe now that she knew I was concerned, she would temper her betting. And I would definitely find alternative locations for relaxation next time we planned a getaway.

"Isn't that wild that the dealer thought you were Holly?" I asked.

Twisting her glass on the drink coaster, she nodded. "I know. We look kind of similar, I guess."

"And if the manager knew her by name, likely she was here on a somewhat regular basis." How far could I probe before I crossed the line? If Fiona weren't involved in this mess, she would ask these questions.

"I must have missed her on my visits," Fiona said. I couldn't imagine and didn't want to know how frequently she came here, or how much money she had gambled. Truly, it was none of my business. But I refused to sit by and let my friend put her future business on the line.

"Fiona." I needed to get this out on the table and let the chips fall where they may.

"I said it's under control," Fiona snapped. We sat back as the server silently placed our steaming plates of orange chicken in front of each of us.

"Can I get either of you anything else?" she asked, looking between us.

Fiona lifted her near empty drink glass. I was counting, and this was actually number three for her in a relatively short amount of time. She had driven us to the casino, but I was preparing to drive home. She glanced at me, eyebrows raised.

Nodding, I said, "I'll drive home." Responding to the server, I said, "Just another water for me. Thanks." Now wasn't the time to further this conversation. The only direction it was likely to go from here was downhill. She knew my position, and I wanted to give her time to ponder and sober up before getting into why she felt the need to gamble with loads of money.

I dove into the crispy chicken covered in orange sauce, certain my stomach would pay me back later for this gut bomb. Fiona was right. It was delicious, a tangy and sweet combo.

"Are you up to talking about Holly?" I asked, hoping to find an agreeable dinner topic. Maybe if I could extend our mealtime, she might decide not to return to the card table, though I could see the allure of the challenge, the sounds and lights of slot machine winners amping up the excitement of possibilities.

"I get what you're doing, Til." Fiona smiled.

Yes, but was it working?

"It is odd that she came here too. Although it's not that far from Belle Harbor," Fiona said.

"What else do you know about her?" I asked, poking another juicy piece of chicken. This truly was one of the tastiest meals I had had. Another casino strategy to keep you coming back.

"She's been an inspector for a while. I don't think her write-ups of the bar were personal because I know several other businesses also had issues with her heavy-handedness."

I scooped several vegetables onto my fork and swirled them in the orange sauce. "Is there any one of them you think could have done this?"

Shaking her head, Fiona said, "Not with any stretch of my imagination."

The server approached to check on us. Thankfully, Fiona declined another drink, although I still planned to drive us home.

"I think we have to consider each of your staff," I said. Until we could rule them out, everyone was on the list. Nobody seemed even close to having a stronger motive than Fiona. It happened in her place of business. And as far as I could tell, she didn't have an alibi. "And the delivery guy." The list continued to grow.

"We need to have a sleuthing sesh at your place," Fiona said. "With your diagramming of everyone and their motive. I just can't be neutral about this."

Agreed. My process of organizing information worked well to highlight and guide us in the right direction. "Let's do it," I said. Scooping the last of the chicken into my mouth, I subtly checked my phone for the time, pondering how I could navigate us to the exit.

"OK. How about a few more rounds, then we get out of here?" Fiona asked.

My shoulders slumped. I knew it was coming, but I had hoped to rescue her before something dire occurred. This was her decision, and she would have to live with the consequences. Sighing, I asked, "Five?" holding up my hand.

"Deal," she said and scooted from the booth to return to the table with Benji. Turning halfway to her destination, she said, "Tilly, this has turned out to be a trip all about me. It doesn't seem like you've had any fun at all." She held her hand out.

"Really, Fiona, I just wanted you to have a break from the stress. I'm good."

She reached out and gave me a quick squeeze. "Love you, my friend."

How good of a friend was I if I couldn't help her? From everyone we listed as suspects, she sat prominently at the top. Motive, means, opportunity. The trifecta of guilt. And Barney had to be thinking along the same lines. My heart said no way could she do this and jeopardize her future. My brain was logically placing the pieces of the puzzle together, and the picture that was forming was frightening.

I followed Fiona back to the card table, hoping with all my strength that she limited the rounds herself before I felt the need to step in. Would this be one of the last excursions with my friend? Barney wasn't above putting friends in jail if the evidence showed he had a case. My thoughts spiraled to ponder who could run her bar. Stacy was a long-time, trusted employee who could likely step in right away if needed.

My friend bounced in her seat, scooting the newly gained chips toward her. She swung around, holding up three fingers. I nodded, relieved she was keeping her commitment.

CHAPTER FIVE

"Tilly, I'm so sorry Fiona is going through this. Is there anything Jack or I could do to help?" Linda asked. My baking partner had become such a good friend. And the fact she was marrying one of my favorite humans on the planet was an incredible blessing for me and him.

I shook my head. "Nah. I don't know what it could be." I moved the empty cupcake pans to the sink for our teenage helper Dexter to take care of when he arrived. Leaning up against the sink, I crossed my arms in front of me. "Linda?"

She turned her head toward me while continuing to wipe down the counter for baking round two. "Yes?"

Dare I say it? My heart couldn't handle thinking about it, let alone uttering the words out loud. "Do you—?" The rest of the sentence couldn't come out of my mouth. I cleared my throat.

Linda placed the towel on the counter and came to face me, taking my hands. "Tilly, believe me. I know how you feel." That she did. With Uncle Jack accused of murdering her former boyfriend and spending several days in jail until they found the actual killer, nobody knew better.

I sniffled and stepped to the side, pacing the length of the kitchen. My pent-up anxiety needed an outlet. "I don't think there is any way Fiona did this. She is so open that I feel like if she was hiding something, it would be noticeable."

She retrieved the towel and continued her cleaning. "I agree. Unfortunately, it's just going to take the time it takes."

"Barney won't make a peep, so I feel like I need to jump in and see what I can find out," I said, stopping to look at Linda.

"Just be careful, Tilly. There's a murderer out there."

I pulled a box from the shelf and folded it up, loading several cupcakes for a delivery to Fiona's. I needed to see for myself how she was doing today. Getting whacked over the head with a bag of frozen ravioli felt personal. If I could find out who might have it in for Holly, it could detract the attention from Fiona.

"I'll be back in a bit. I need to see her in person this morning," I said, heading out to the boardwalk. Sure, she was carefree last night. But being plied with drinks and the festive atmosphere of the casino, she likely masked her emotions. Facing reality when she arrived at the scene of the crime today could be a whole different story.

The day was still early enough that a cool breeze hit my face. I certainly needed the wake up after little sleep. A few beach goers had their coffees in hand to greet the day. It wouldn't be long before the place filled with families making memories. Hopefully they were all oblivious to the murder at Fiona's. It hadn't even occurred to me until just now that word would get out and her business could take a big hit for quite a while. That could also be a downward spiral of finances for her expansion and possibly keep the doors from opening at all.

As I neared the end of the boardwalk, my pulse raced and my pace quickened. The door to Fiona's was open and I could hear music, portending a promising scene.

Entering, I heard voices and saw Fiona and Stacy behind the bar. I approached them, lifting the box and holding it out. "Brought goodies," I said and placed it on the bar, opening the lid.

"Thanks!" Stacy said, grabbing a napkin and diving in.

"You're not fooling me," Fiona said, grinning.

I didn't expect I would, but it was a good excuse. Leading Fiona away from the bar, I quietly asked how she was doing. Her outward exuberance belied her droopy eyes. I gave her a quick squeeze and sat in a booth, gesturing for her to join me. She glanced over her shoulder at Stacy, who continued to munch on the pastry and prep at the bar. I knew for myself that keeping busy helped distract from reality, at least for a short amount of time. Plus we both had businesses to run.

"Just a few minutes, then I'll jet," I said. Now was too soon to revisit her excesses last night. She had enough on her plate.

"Tilly, I'm really worried," she muttered. "Not about being accused. But word will travel and my business will take a hit, regardless of my innocence." She leaned in. "If it goes on for very long, I might have to let people go. That's what's really eating me up."

"What can I do?" My muscles tensed, and I hurt for my friend.

She pursed her lips and shook her head. "Just what you are. Being a friend. Sorry for getting carried away last night."

"I understand. Hey, if you want a thrill and total escape, why don't you come with Justin and me the next time we go to the comedy club? You can do open mic." Convinced she would jump at my brilliant brainstorm, I was a little hurt when she laughed it off. But I got it. That type of vulnerability wasn't for everyone.

"Fiona?" Stacy approached the table. "Ronnie called out again. What do you want me to do?"

Fiona balled her fists. She did not need the added stress. I was incredibly grateful for my reliable team of Linda and Dexter at the bakery. "OK. Call Kris to see if she can come in for at least a few hours."

Stacy turned and headed back to the bar. "Oh, that guy!" Fiona clasped her hands together so hard her knuckles turned white. She had a pretty good crew. I was sorry to see a rotten apple was spoiling the bunch.

From the bar area, Stacy yelled over that Kris was available and would be here.

Sighing, Fiona said, "Well, one crisis averted. I'm going to have to let Ronnie go. He's excellent at his job but is so unreliable. I just don't get that."

You could teach people skills, but behavior was a different story. "Sorry about that. But if it's less stress for you that he's gone, then it's the right decision."

"When it rains, it pours," Fiona said and leaned in again, lowering her voice. "Stacy has been with me the longest of anyone. And I trust her with everything. But lately she's been flaking out."

The final straw that might send Fiona over the edge would be if something happened with her most trusted employee. I waited to see if she would reveal anything else. If I knew more, maybe I could help. Desperate to get my friend back to her normal, peppy self, I prompted, "Oh?"

Keeping her voice low, she continued, "She's going through a divorce and really hurting for money."

OK. Other than Stacy's attention away from the bar, I didn't see Fiona's concern. If Stacy needed the job, I would expect she might want the extra hours. When people were desperate, especially when it came to finances, they could make rash decisions. What wasn't Fiona sharing? Now was not the time to delve into a discussion about Stacy with her in the room, but some underlying worry was on Fiona's mind.

"Fiona," I said.

She vehemently shook her head. "No, Tilly. She could never do that." She scooted to the edge of the booth. "I just can't go there." Standing, she held out her arms.

I hugged her tightly. She had so much on her mind. I had to figure out how to help. My friend's pain was mine.

CHAPTER SIX

I really needed some Unkie time. The rest of my day after leaving Fiona's was wrecked. I struggled to focus on anything, going through the motions to prep the baking for the next day. My night was just as restless, so I expected today to be a blur. Unkie always had a pot of coffee going so he was ready to chat up anyone who came into Checkered Past Antiques.

It seemed eons ago when he had carved out a corner of his shop for my first bakery kitchen. If not for his support and encouragement, I wouldn't have my dream life in Belle Harbor. Even though sometimes the encouragement came as a kick in the tush, and appropriately needed, it was always done in love. Uncle Jack was my surrogate mom and dad since my folks lived on the other side of the continent.

Entering the brightly lit store, I spotted Unkie with his head in a box, where it looked like he was unloading several new pieces. "Hey there," I hollered, hoping not to startle him too badly.

He swung his head around, grinning from ear to ear. He set the small ceramic owl in a space on the table and greeted me with open arms. "Hey yourself." He reached up and moved a piece of hair from in front of my eyes. "Darlin', did you even sleep at all last night?"

Unkie turned and headed back to the coffee corner, waving at me to join him. "I don't know what to do." I plopped into a chair while he poured me a cup and set it on the table next to me.

"I know you know this, but it does no good to Fiona if you aren't taking care of yourself." He blew on the coffee and sipped it.

Bowing my head, I sniffled. "I know." I grabbed a tissue from the table and wiped my eyes, stuttering a breath. "She's devastated."

"Look. I know it's hard to hear, but it's going to take some time," Unkie said.

"Yeah, and you of all people know how patient I am."

"Not," he replied as we both chuckled. "Right now, just being close to your friend is probably the best thing you can do."

Reaching for my cup, I hesitated. "Has Barney said anything to you?" My question slightly tipped open Pandora's box.

Unkie shook his head. "Nah. And I haven't asked yet. It's still early."

I inhaled to steady my breathing and heart rate. "Moving onto a happier subject." Unkie and Linda's wedding was happening next week. Would Fiona be able to attend? What if things took a turn and Barney had to put her in jail? Quickly shaking my head to jettison those thoughts, I continued, "What else do you and Linda need? You have your tux, right?"

Standing up and saluting me, he said, "Yes, ma'am!"

"Good. Neither of us wants Linda thinking about any last-minute details," I said, standing to hug him. I laid my head on his shoulder for a few extra seconds, taking in the comfort.

"Hey," he said, releasing me and approaching one of his tables. He moved several pieces around, an old cuckoo clock, a glass decanter that looked like it was used for very expensive liquor, and a small brass-framed mirror. He rounded the table, bending to look under, and continued to move pieces.

"What are you looking for?"

He stepped back, hands on hips, brows furrowed. My mind immediately went to concern for Unkie's memory. Did he forget something he had previously done? His mind was as sharp as those half his age, but you never knew.

"That antique phone," he said, moving to other tables in the shop. "Maybe someone moved it." He circled the store, returning to the place he started, and looked me straight in the eye. "I think I've been robbed."

Wandering the aisles, I followed the same path he had walked, scouring the stacks of antiques for the phone. I knew exactly which one he referred to, because for a period of time it would randomly ring, like someone from long ago calling the present. It wasn't here.

I had to ask: "Are you sure you didn't sell it?"

"No, I didn't. And my memory is just fine!" He huffed.

I held up a halting hand in surrender. "You need to let Barney know."

Until now, Checkered Past Antiques and my bakery were two of the few places not yet hit by burglars. It seemed no one was safe.

"That really peeves me!" He pulled out his phone and began typing, I assumed, to inform Barney of another theft. Lifting his head up, he stuffed his phone into his pocket. "Argh!" He headed to the front door and ran his hand up and down the jam, searching for damage. "Dang." He turned back toward me. "I have no idea how they got in."

Reaching under the counter at the cash registers, I pulled out a notebook and pen, handing them to Unkie. "You should look around to see what else might be missing." I had no earthly idea how he could tell. At one time I had helped him with some organization of the items in his shop, but it appeared there was no rhyme or reason to what was where—though he always seemed to know exactly where to find things in the jumble.

Snatching the notebook, he replied, "Yeah. That's a good idea." He returned to the coffee corner and plopped into a chair, placing the notebook on the table and rubbing his hands on his pants.

Something else was on his mind. Normally, Unkie was even-keeled, even in the face of drama. I followed him back to resume our chat and see if I could pry it out of his stoic manner. Rarely did he want to trouble anyone else with his needs. "Spill it."

Shaking his head, he chuckled. "You, almost more than anyone else, get me." He stood. Everything had been going so well. Was he about to lay some bad news on me? I was sure it wasn't about his and Linda's relationship. He was aging. Was there a health issue that had emerged? I couldn't take it if Unkie wasn't here. In a relatively short amount of time, he had become an integral part of my life. He stepped in front of me. "I have something to ask you. And of course you can say no. And it won't hurt my feelings. Too much."

This slow walking me to what he was going to say was going to make my head explode. "You're scaring me. What is it?" I stood just a few feet from him, glaring into his eyes.

His smile overtook his entire face.

OK, Tilly. It can't be all that bad. I reached out and put my hand on his arm.

Unkie took both of my hands in his. "I know it's a bit unorthodox. But hey." He placed his hand over his heart. "Would you be my attendant at the wedding? My best niece, so to speak?"

I slowly backed up and sat. In a million years, I couldn't have predicted that question. But I would take it every time over other not so good news.

"What about Barney?" Wasn't it customary for your best friend to be your best man?

Waving off my question, Unkie replied, "The old coot will be just fine. Probably glad not to be in the limelight."

Reaching for a tissue from the table, I dabbed the forming tears. "Of course I will. Anything for you!"

Unkie wrapped his arms around me and squeezed. "Enough mush."

Yeah, that was probably his quota for the decade, and there would be enough coming up at the wedding.

"You should get to work on that list. It might be helpful to have it for the community meeting tonight." The mayor had convened a special session specifically to cover the rash of robberies and how they planned to deal with them. The only thing I could think of was more security, and that would cost more money. But something had to be done before tourism declined.

CHAPTER SEVEN

I was still riding the high of Uncle Jack's request to be his attendant at the wedding. There was no better honor than to show how much I loved him and to show my pure joy at his and Linda's marriage. I needed that boost to my mood with all the other troubles plaguing Fiona and the local businesses. Entering the double doors to the community center, I scanned the throng of bodies, looking for Uncle Jack. From across the room, he held up a hand, surrounded by several people like he was holding court.

The room was packed, and I doubted there would be enough chairs to seat all attendees. Recent events had everyone on alert and concerned for our safety. I approached Unkie, who was eating something that looked like pudding from a small plastic bowl. Those huddled with him also had a bowl in their hands that, from what I could see, were filled with samples provided by a new business in town, Just Desserts.

Raising my eyebrows at Unkie as he wove through the crowd toward me, I said, "Traitor."

He licked both sides of the spoon and threw it and the empty bowl into the trash. Seeing a brown smudge on his cheek, I grabbed a napkin and dabbed the extra food on his face. "Just checking out the competition," he said, taking the napkin and wiping the rest of his face.

"And?"

Nodding, he replied, "Pretty good." We turned to scout out empty chairs and were stuck with two along the perimeter of the room. "That was avocado coconut cream mousse."

Thankfully, that was not one of my treats at Luna's Bakery and Cafe, so no competition there. "Sounds yummy." I stood, waving as I spotted Fiona enter the room. Not sure whether to expect her, I was pleased she came. She belonged here, and hopefully it might quell some rumors of her guilt if she was willing to be seen in public. The volume of the chatter significantly decreased as she made her way to us. I hugged her, and she took the seat on the other side of Unkie.

"Glad to see you, my dear." Uncle Jack had known Fiona much longer than I, and he considered her family.

The gavel loudly banged at the front of the room where Hazel, the town council president, stood behind the podium. Several more taps and her desired result realized with attendees taking their seats. "I want to welcome you to this special session of our council meeting. You all know why we're here." Her gazed drifted toward us and landed on Fiona.

Oh, I wanted to sprint to the front of the room and gavel her to defend my friend but thought better of it with Barney sitting right there.

"We have the police chief here to start us off with an update on the murder," Hazel said, dragging out the last word and returning her line of sight right on Fiona. Barney stood, and Hazel added, "After that, we'll talk about what we can do about the robberies."

Hazel grinned widely at Barney, like she was gritting her teeth. I don't think she approved of her sister Florence dating him, but as a prominent local politician, and given Barney's job, she had to act the part of the accepting sibling. She stretched out her arm to hand him the gavel, and he shook his head, moving to the podium. A small smattering of applause prompted him to hold up a halting hand.

"I won't take up too much of your time." He paused. "I know you're curious, and I'll tell you what I can."

You could hear a pin drop. What was he about to reveal? Neither Fiona nor I had gotten an update yet. I clasped my hands together, squeezing tight to contain my anxiety. What if he was about to share something that would incriminate Fiona? I closed my eyes, preparing for the worst. He wouldn't do it here, would he?

"We are still investigating and gathering information. I appreciate everyone's cooperation so far, and I'm confident we'll solve this," he said, pausing again. "I can't take questions, but I will keep you up to date."

I opened my eyes, releasing the breath I didn't realize I was holding. OK. That wasn't bad. Really, that wasn't anything. I was certain Barney knew more than he said. I pondered how I could pry into the details.

Hazel stood, tilting her head and gushing over Barney's statement. "Thank you so much, Chief. Of course, we're counting on you to keep us safe." Again, her glance landed on Fiona.

As I scooted to the edge of my chair, Uncle Jack gently placed his hand on my back. *Unkie, I know.* I would not do anything, but geez, Hazel! I couldn't stand that woman, stemming from the first time I met her during the annual Arts Walk. Her dissing of Unkie's store was over the top.

Slamming the gavel so hard the crowd jumped in unison, Hazel addressed the group. "Now, let's start with some information. You know how I love data." The Hazel show continued. Waving the gavel from left to right, she continued, "Everyone who has been a victim of theft, can you please stand?"

Most of the crowd shuffled to their feet as I heard gasps. This was worse than I thought.

"Thank you. That's what I was afraid of," Hazel said. "Be seated." She pointed the gavel as if it was an extension of her arm.

I was one of the few business owners who remained seated, if not the only one. Was I next in line or was there something about the bakery not worth the trouble? We had a lot of expensive specialty baking equipment. But that stuff's heavy and it would be hard to pawn.

Hazel moved the meeting along by gathering any additional details from the owners that might help with the investigation. Time of day, what was taken, any pattern of which ones were hit. Did the burglar have a grand plan they were following? Barney and his deputy were furiously taking notes. This mass interview strategy helped to gather a lot of information in a small amount of time.

My head bowed, and I took notes, planning to do my own analysis. With this many data points, there was a story here, and I wanted to find it.

George, the owner of the moped rental shop, stood and raised his voice. "Enough of this government mumbo jumbo! What are you going to do about it?"

Following that lead, several others raised from their seats and chimed in.

Barney approached the podium, attempting to quell the impending riot. Hazel tucked the gavel close to her, refusing to let anyone else touch it. Barney held out his hand. "I know you're angry. We all are. But we have to stick together to solve this. You are our eyes and ears out there."

"And what about her?" George swiveled and jabbed his arm in Fiona's direction. "The murder and the burglaries are somehow related."

Stepping away from the podium and walking a few steps toward George, Barney said, "We don't know that. And it does no one any good to start rumors."

Getting the message to stifle it, George plopped down into his seat, quieting the crowd.

From my peripheral vision, I saw Fiona's head fall into her hands. The accusations devastated her. Uncle Jack stood and grabbed Fiona's hand. "Let's go. We're done here."

I fell in behind them as we navigated around the people seated in the extra chairs toward the door, making a dramatic exit.

I certainly hoped the meeting had been fruitful for Barney because it did more damage to Fiona. The question that remained from George was at the forefront of my brain. Was there a connection between Holly's murder and the burglaries?

CHAPTER EIGHT

Sleep eluded me most of the night. The revelation that the burglaries might be related to the murder parked at the forefront of my brain, blocking most every other thought from existence. This might just crack the case wide open and allow some progress, enlightening an entire other dimension to the picture.

Justin had retrieved me from the bakery and led me by the hand to a stop at Mocha Joe's before we ventured up the mountain to the wedding venue. "Tilly, I want to give your brain the space to process that new info, but if you want to talk about it . . ."

He was an excellent partner to bounce ideas off of because he took a more neutral stance. Heavens knew I was emotionally attached to the case and might be seeing nothing clearly.

"OK. How about on our drive up there?" I said.

Squeezing my hand, he used his other to open the door to the coffee place. Even in the late afternoon, this place was packed. Someday soon, I would have to quiz Joe on his marketing strategies. While my bakery did well, we definitely had lulls in our day. Justin pulled me close, and I leaned my head on his shoulder, feeling the calm and comfort. If I didn't relax at least a little, I knew my stressed brain wouldn't be able to think.

Silently edging forward for our turn at the counter, I began at the beginning. Maybe looking at the pieces separately and seeing commonalities would illuminate a correlation. Fiona had been at the bakery early the day of Holly's murder. Certainly, there was friction between them. Enough for a motive for murder? If I put a stranger in place of Fiona, maybe that would ease up my thoughts to consider scenarios. Let's name the killer Artie. If Artie got mad enough, could the situation have gotten out of hand? Maybe Artie defended himself with the frozen ravioli?

"Look at you two." Mocha Joe's greeting jostled me from my thoughts. "If I didn't know any better, I'd think you were the happy couple soon to be married."

Releasing my hand, Justin pulled his wallet from his pocket. He chuckled and got his card out, ready to swipe through the reader.

"Justin?" I prompted.

He slowly turned to look at me, the top of his ears beet red. Joe had really struck a nerve. That wasn't the first round of teasing we had received about getting married, and it likely wouldn't be the last. I had given up trying to predict where our relationship would go. Mostly. One of my goals was to focus on enjoying the moments.

Snickering, Justin said, "Guess we should order first."

I looked at Joe and smirked. Justin was one of the most relaxed and chill people I knew, but that certainly threw him for a loop. We ordered coffees and pastries to go and stepped to the side to wait for it to be ready. Grabbing Justin's hand again, I squeezed to hopefully help him release some of that anxiety.

"Joe?" I flicked my head slightly in the direction of the end of the counter. None other than Ronnie wore an apron and was preparing coffee.

Glancing in Ronnie's direction, Joe stepped forward and lowered his voice. "I know."

"Are you sure?" I asked. Without knowing the details of Ronnie's firing by Fiona, I was still concerned for Joe's business. Fiona was generous but also a shrewd businesswoman. I only hoped Ronnie hadn't conned his way in.

"He's on a trial period. I'm trying to mentor him to be successful. I'm all about second chances, but he knows he's on a short leash," Joe said.

Did Fiona know about this? Or provide any kind of reference to Joe? Granted, sometimes a position just wasn't the right fit for a person. Ronnie was darting around, quickly filling orders, and seemed to fit in. I sincerely hoped this would work out.

Justin and I stepped aside. "I have an idea about how we can approach the sleuthing on our trip," I said. The drive to the lodge was about an hour each way, sufficient time to exhaust all theories, and then some.

"OK," he muttered, reaching for our order as the server placed the tray on the counter.

I retrieved the keys from my backpack, and we exited the shop and headed to the parking lot. Fiona had agreed to loan me her car until I could find time to go with Justin to get my own. I had it all picked out and couldn't wait to get my little mini-Cooper.

"Justin," I said. "I hope Joe's teasing didn't bother you." I was in no hurry to get married. If that were to happen, it would be all in good time.

He fussed with the coffee tray, moving the pastry bags around. Something was distracting him, and it seemed to be more than the ribbing from Joe. I unlocked the doors and saw the passenger seat filled with papers. Justin put the coffee on the roof of the car, scooping the papers into a pile. He stood, looking at something in his hand. "Tilly?"

Seated behind the wheel, I said, "Yes?"

He leaned into the car and handed me the papers, tapping the one on top. "I hate to be nosy," he started, grabbing the coffee and taking a seat.

An inspection report for Fiona's bar from Holly dated two days before her murder, red pen all over it with many critical violations. "Justin, it can't be."

He slammed the door, which caused me to drop the papers. "That level would have required Fiona to completely shut down the bar," he said.

"I know," I said, my hands dropping to my lap as I gazed out the window. My pulse raced, with Fiona returning to the top of the suspect list. I just couldn't go there.

Justin took the papers and placed them in the backseat. "I don't think we should jump to any conclusions."

"You're right. I know Holly was vindictive for some reason. Maybe if we uncover that, we might glean more clues." But what explanation could there be? For the first time, I pondered the prospect that Fiona was more involved than she let on. Was she too scared to share what happened? If there had been an argument, maybe it had gotten out of hand and Fiona had grabbed the closest thing to her. Had Holly come at Fiona, who was just defending herself? I started the car, still in a daze from this newfound information. So many questions. I needed to talk to Fiona directly and get the truth.

For the hourlong drive to the resort, Justin and I said few words. My brain wove through several routes, trying to devise a logical explanation for Fiona's involvement. None of the resulting pictures was good.

"Tilly," Justin broke the silence as we entered the gravel parking lot. The mountains loomed large to my left, a stunning backdrop for a wedding.

I pulled the car into a spot and turned off the key, the engine quietly clicking as it cooled. I reached for my backpack in the back seat to get my notebook as I stuttered with a sob. "Justin, I can't lose her." In the relatively short time I had been in Belle Harbor, Fiona had befriended me and we had become as close as sisters.

"I know," he said, placing a hand on my shoulder. "I'm confident there's a logical explanation. You have to believe that."

If only. I exited the car to the refreshing mountain air and stared at the lodge. I inhaled deeply to shift my focus to our purpose at hand. To make sure Linda and Unkie's wedding was everything they deserved,

I had to give this trip my full attention. Justin and I entered the lodge for our meeting with the manager. Fiona's troubles would have to wait for another time.

CHAPTER NINE

"Tilly, I'm so sorry this happened to you." Linda swept the piles of dry ingredients strewn on the floor into an enormous pile. I held the dustpan to scoop another batch to deposit into the trash. I had so hoped that we might escape the prolific burglar, but no such luck. The only thing I could see that was missing were several day-old cupcakes. And I was grateful that nobody was hurt. We certainly had valuables in the bakery, but lifting and fencing mixers and other large bakery appliances probably wouldn't be very fruitful.

"I was prepared in case it did. Thankfully, most of the damage is just a mess to clean up," I said, standing back to assess the rest of our task.

Linda stepped forward with her hands on the top of the broom. "I wonder if they are a homeless person," she said, her brows furrowing.

"All I know is my head is spinning trying to figure out any rhyme or reason to what's going on." I moved to the trash can and pulled out the full plastic bag and tied it off, placing it next to the two we had already filled near the back door. "I guess that could be, given that they stole food." But why would they turn this place upside down if they only wanted food? What was I missing? I estimated the remainder of the disarray would fill two more garbage bags. I pulled on the handle of the door leading to the alley. There was no damage around it to show they had broken in. Had someone accidentally left it unlocked? The front door was also undamaged, leaving me baffled as to how they got in.

The door slowly opened with my hand on it, causing my heart to jump. Our resident teenager poked his curly-haired head through, gazing around the kitchen. I stepped back, letting Dexter in.

"What happened?" he said, heading to the center of the room, spinning around, taking in the remainder of the evidence of the break-in. Sweeping his arm to the ceiling, he continued, "Tilly, no."

Shaking my head, I said, "It's OK, Dexter. Nobody was hurt. They only took some cupcakes as far as we can tell."

Circling the kitchen, he said, "It's not OK." He was right. Stopping in front of the refrigerator and peering through the glass door at the empty trays where the cupcakes used to be, he opened the door. I expected he was in shock, taking in the unusual circumstances. I ran my hand along the smooth stainless-steel counter, feeling more grit from the remaining sugar. Grabbing a wet towel, I swiped along the surface, attempting to wipe away this experience.

"Dexter, we've got a double order to get ready this morning for that grand opening of the new kite shop," I said, hoping to divert all of us to a more practical focus than wallowing in this mess.

Sighing, he stepped back. "I hope they catch the scum who's been doing this."

I looked at Linda and smirked.

"We couldn't agree more," she said, taking Dexter's backpack and hanging it up near the back door. "Let's wrap this up and get to baking."

His cheeks drooped. "Tilly, do you know any more about what's happening?" This was really bothering him.

I moved the two mixers into place for our first batch and got out the recipe card for the cream-filled cupcakes. "I don't. But Barney is coming in a bit to take a report. We can see if he'll share an update with us."

Dexter silently retrieved all the ingredients, moving like a robot for the mechanical task of mixing the batter. "Oh, I almost forgot." He scooted back from the counter as I handed him an apron. "I was wondering if I could leave early from my next shift. I'm going to that gamer con."

Linda had stashed the broom and final pile from our morning mess. "What's that?" she said, looking between Dexter and me.

"Yeah. So us online gamers go to these cons to meet the people that make the games, and there's all kinds of stuff they sell, and they have contests and—" Dexter bounced up and down on his tiptoes like he was preparing to bound across the room.

Holding up her hand as she bent over, Linda chuckled. "You must really enjoy it. So con is convention?"

"Oh. Yep," he replied. Dexter regaled us regularly with his conquests in the online gaming world that had something to do with football. His local friends played, along with people across the world. "I'm really hoping to meet Slaya65 in person this time. He's in the top three almost every season. I need to get some tips from him."

Not understanding this other world, I could only imagine what Dexter was describing. When he talked about it, his eyes sparkled. He kept us on our toes and in touch with what was going on with the youth of the community.

The door to the kitchen from the lobby swung open with a knock. "Hey everyone," Barney said. He pointed at me. "Tilly, you really should keep the front door locked when you're back here."

"Yeah. Probably a good idea, at least until our official opening time." I wanted to be the go-to place people would come to, even before the sun came up. I hated how one person could ruin things for everyone else.

"What's going on? How am I the last person to hear?!" Unkie burst through the door and beelined to Linda, wrapping her in a bear hug. Turning, he approached me, head tipped with an admonishing look. "Tilly," he said and came in for a squeeze.

"Unkie, we're fine. They just left a mess to clean up." I glanced around, thankful he hadn't seen the extent of it to set him off even further.

"Jack, let the police do our job," Barney said, moving to the middle of the room. "I'm getting a report."

"Report!" Jack said. "What good is that going to do to catch this bugger?"

Linda sidled next to Unkie and slyly clasped his hand. Turning to her, he tipped his head with a tight-lipped smile.

I was sure Barney was grateful for that de-escalation technique. He took out his notebook and silently began writing. We all waited while he kept his head bowed. In his own world, Dexter had continued prepping the cupcakes, lining the pans and starting up the first mixer. The sound startled us all as I squeaked, "Ah!" Bless his heart for soldiering on as us adults were too distracted.

Slapping his hand over the top of his head, Dexter said, "I'm so sorry. Should I not be doing this?" He backed up and paced over to the empty refrigerator and back. "I'm just so out of sorts. I don't know what to do."

I put my hand on his shoulder. "You're doing what you should be doing." Looking at everyone else in the room, I flung my head toward the door. We needed to move on with business as usual. I gestured for Barney and Unkie to wrap it up and head out.

"OK. But-" Unkie started. I held up my hand. His shoulders dropped, and he gave Linda a peck on the cheek.

CHAPTER TEN

I placed a hand on Dexter's shoulder. "You're doing a great job. And yes, you can leave early."

His hand hovered over the on switch for the mixer. He turned toward me, jowls sagging. "Are you sure? Maybe if I was here earlier, I could have caught the burglar." He dropped his arm to his side.

Backing away, I shook my head. "In no uncertain terms should you ever think about trying to catch them." Who was I to talk? Always poking my nose into everyone's business, my natural curiosity driving a need to know. I glanced at Linda, who busied herself prepping our lunch ingredients. She had a pile of diced vegetables for our salads and loaded the ingredients into the to-go containers. The violation of someone coming in here uninvited and making a colossal mess of this place was unnerving. I wasn't so concerned about the financial loss, but the potential for encountering someone in the act frightened me. I got the feeling we arrived not long after they had left. If they were just hungry, I would have given them food. Placing my hand on my chest to quell my rising pulse, I said, "Dexter, Barney will figure this out."

"I know," he said, his head still hanging. I had not expected this upbeat kid to be hit so hard with the burglary. In a short time, he had become part of our family. I wanted to find a way for him to feel safe. For us all to feel safe. The continued burglaries with no apparent progress had all the business owners on edge. Hearing Barney's voice in my head, I pushed it aside, vowing to do my own investigation. What could it hurt if I just asked a few questions? His police department didn't have enough staff to keep up with all the incidents. There just had to be a pattern we weren't seeing.

"Go ahead," I encouraged Dexter to continue with the mixing. Routine tasks would help us return as much as possible to normal.

Linda had silently prepared all the items for round two of baking. Our little team ran like a well-oiled machine. I grabbed another wet towel and finished wiping down the remainder of the mess left by the intruder. The hum of the kitchen operations provided a level of calm as I headed to the lobby to prepare for our customer opening.

With her hand shading her eyes outside the front door, Fiona peered in. Seeing me, she waved and entered. "Hi girl." She beelined for a hug. Her peppy exterior belied her underlying stress, clear from the dark circles under her eyes. I squeezed her firmly, hoping this was a surprise good news visit. With Fiona's late-night schedule, she was typically not up and about at this early hour.

Grabbing her hand, I led her to a booth along the window. "What's up?" I asked, peering into her eyes for any clue about her random appearance at the cafe.

"Can't I just stop by for a hello to my bestie?"

My shoulders dropped. "Of course," I said.

Looking past me toward the kitchen door, she said, "I heard about your break-in. Are you OK?"

I nodded. "Yes. A little unnerving, but mostly it was just a mess. Probably hard to hawk a large mixing machine at the pawnshop."

"Glad to see you have a sense of humor," she said, gazing around, fidgeting with her hands in her lap.

"I don't know how to bring this up without sounding like your mom," I started.

She snapped her head back to face me.

I gulped. Was I about to jeopardize my friendship? And for what? Butting myself into her business? She obviously was a regular at the casino and didn't seem to be any worse for the wear.

Sitting back, I put the towel on the table and moved it around.

"I know what you're going to say. And I should have been the one to bring it up in the first place."

Was our friendship going to be OK?

"I just wish there was something more I could do," I offered.

"You are my friend. And I know everything you do and say is out of love," she said. "I couldn't ask for anything more."

"Fiona—"

"You were right to call me out the other night. I enjoy the casino, and blowing off steam, but I went too far."

Reaching my hand across the table, I said, "Fiona, I know it's taking time. But they will resolve it before we know it."

She pulled her fist up to her nose and sniffled. "Tilly, what if it's not? They need someone to be accountable. And the obvious person is me."

Exiting the booth, I moved to sit next to Fiona and pulled her close. "You can't think that way." I was now more determined than ever to sleuth out any clues I could. As soon as Dexter and Linda had things under control, I had to escape for my errand. Maybe a distraction would help. "You won't believe what Justin did when we visited the wedding venue yesterday."

Fiona sniffed and turned toward me.

Taking that as a good sign, I continued. My face warmed as I relived his gesture.

"Tilly, why are you blushing? This must be good!"

Mission accomplished. "After we confirmed all the plans for Unkie and Linda's wedding, we were on the deck of the resort, chatting about nothing. He spontaneously gets down on one knee in front of me, taking my hand."

Fiona slapped her hand over her mouth, her eyes bulging.

Holding up my hand, I said, "No, no, no. He was just joking."

"Was he?"

"Well, he didn't have a ring."

"Tilly, you know it's just a matter of time. Oh, I can't wait."

I scooted out of the booth and retrieved the towel to wipe down all the surfaces in the lobby. While I knew Justin wasn't serious with his mock proposal, it felt like a dry run. I wasn't sure how to feel about it. Don't get me wrong, I had envisioned the moment many times. I ran through all the reasons in my head why I would say no, none of them legitimate. He was kind, hard-working, supportive of me, fun to be with, and easy on the eyes. My heart raced.

"One wedding at a time," I said.

Fiona joined me and said, "I should let you get back to work. Thank you." Tears puddled in the corners of her eyes. I couldn't imagine how hard this must be, having the accusations hanging over her head. With a last hug, she stuttered in a breath and left.

Oh, my friend. This couldn't go on any longer. I poked my head into the kitchen to check on my crew. Linda waved me over.

"How's he doing?" I asked.

She shrugged. "OK, I guess."

I scanned the room, and it appeared they had everything under control. "Can you survive without me for a bit?"

Linda smiled. "Of course. I figured you needed to go, so we've got it handled."

I retrieved my backpack from the hook by the door and replaced it with my apron. "I'll try to be back as soon as I can. I really appreciate it."

Dexter whipped his head in our direction and said, "Go get 'em Tilly!"

Chuckling at my cheering section, I looped the backpack strap over my shoulder and headed out through the lobby. I would try to hit as many shops as fast as I could, figuring the more data I had, the more likely I might see a pattern. I dug into my backpack to confirm my notebook had plenty of paper and that I had a couple of pens. Leaving the cafe, I gazed out at the gently rolling waves. The morning weather was calm with little wind and the sun showing beyond the hills behind the boardwalk. Another perfect day in Belle Harbor, except for the massive cloud of suspicion hanging over Fiona. Like a student on their first day of school, I bounded off to learn everything I could.

CHAPTER ELEVEN

My first stop would be the new kite shop that was just beginning their business—one of the first to be hit, even before their grand opening. I hoped the burglary wouldn't deter or delay their opening. The lights blazed through the front windows, all covered with a brightly colored display of kites, throwing a rainbow reflection onto the sidewalk.

"Knock, knock," I said, entering to the sound of upbeat music playing in the background. Note to self: consider adding music to jazz up the vibe at the cafe.

"Welcome," came the voice from behind the counter. "Just a sec."

I looked around at the variety of beach gear available for purchase, from small plastic buckets and shovels to highly intricate and advanced kites that looked like they might take an engineer to run.

Emerging into view, a middle-aged man approached me with his arm extended. "I'm Michael," he said. "What can I do for you?"

Uncle Jack was always current with the comings and goings of Belle Harbor, especially anything to do with businesses. He had already met Michael and gave me the lowdown on him and his shop.

I met his hand, and we shook. "Hi, Michael. I'm Tilly. Owner of Luna's Bakery and Cafe." I pointed in the direction of my business, which I was sure he already knew the location of.

"Oh, I have to get there soon. I hear great things," he said.

I felt my face warm, still not quite believing that I had a successful bakery. "Your first order is on me. Try our signature cream-filled cupcakes. You'll be hooked."

"That's what I'm afraid of." He chuckled, patting his stomach. "Are you looking for something specific?"

I pulled out my notebook and turned to a blank page, tapping it with my pen. "Kind of." Re-considering my decision to barge in and start quizzing someone who didn't know me, I hesitated.

"Looks like you came prepared for something," he said.

I did. Hoping my nosiness didn't get us started on the wrong foot, I began, "I apologize if this is too intrusive, but I'm fed up with the burglaries. I'm just asking around to see if I can discover any pattern."

Michael leaned back against the counter, crossing his arms over his mid-section. "Isn't that the job of the police?"

Defenses up, I resigned myself to no further progress with Michael. How could I gracefully extricate myself and not damage this relationship? Bakery treats usually smoothed things over. I kicked myself for not thinking about leading with that strategy.

Slipping my backpack from my shoulder to the floor, I bent to unzip and return my notebook and pen. "Well, if you think of anything, please be sure to let the police know."

"I will," Michael said, moving toward the door.

"Thank you," I said over my shoulder as I exited. Never hurts to be polite. Perhaps he would reconsider after he gave it some thought.

"Tilly?" Pivoting, I saw him continue to hold the door open.

Smiling, I braced for more scolding, trying anyway I could to soften him up.

"Thanks for the concern and what you're doing. I've just seen more trouble come from vigilantes sometimes than the criminals themselves," he said, stepping from the store to the sidewalk, letting the door close behind him.

"I get that. I'm just so burned up about this. Partly because my friend Fiona is intertwined in this somehow with the death of the inspector happening at her bar. I really just want to help her too."

Again folding his arms over his chest, he continued, "For what it's worth, I think my burglary happened between two and six in the morning."

Quickly retrieving my notebook, I scribbled down that detail. "That's so helpful." I reached out my arm and shook hands. "Thank you."

Michael retreated into his store as I exhaled a deep breath. That was more intense than I expected. I was so task-oriented sometimes I forget to focus on the relationship side. Definitely a batch of cupcakes in Michael's future.

Next up was Daffy Taffy. The owner and I had met before and were on friendly terms, so my optimism soared at prospects of digging up more clues. Opening the door, I saw Justice with a cart loaded with several buckets of different taffy flavors. The machine in the back room whirred, pulling more of the sugary candy to keep the tubes full. Taffy was Unkie's weakness. OK, one of his sweet treat weaknesses. I probably shouldn't indulge him with any taffy today, especially so close to the wedding. His tux fit beautifully as it was, and he didn't need the extra stress of getting another one at the last minute.

"Hi Justice," I said, hoping I didn't startle her too much. Her door didn't have a bell at the entry like my cafe to alert her when people entered. She always had a steady stream of customers, much like Mocha Joe, so it would go off all the time.

She whipped her head around, her long, dark hair fanning out as she faced me, scooping the taffy from the bucket into the tube—sour apple, one of my favorites, along with the spicier cinnamon hots. Justice was a tall, young beauty who ran the family store with a smile on her face and a kind word for all. She dropped the scoop into her bucket and wiped her hands on her apron.

"Tilly, good to see you." She raised her voice over the hum of the taffy-pulling machine. She drew her eyebrows together and continued, "Don't tell me." She shook her head.

I glanced around, glad there wasn't obvious mayhem left by the burglar. "Sadly, yes. Earlier this morning."

"I'm so sorry." She stepped closer to me.

"That's actually why I'm here." I retrieved my notebook. "They left a mess and took some cupcakes, as far as I can tell."

"I'll do anything I can to help. This has got to stop," she said.

I couldn't agree more. "I know Barney wouldn't approve, but I'm convinced the burglaries are related to Holly's murder."

"And you have to do what you can to help your friend. I get it."

"Do you know what time they broke in?" I started.

Returning to the cart with the buckets, Justice continued filling the tubes with the wrapped taffy. "If I don't keep up on this, we'll run out before the end of the day. Go ahead. I can multitask."

"Most every shop is closed by late evening until early morning, so it's prime picking for a burglar. I just can't figure out what they're looking for," I said.

She worked her way down the aisle. "Yep, same."

"We deposit any cash we receive at the end of every day. So the most valuable thing at the bakery is the equipment. I don't get it," I said.

"Just like us. What are we missing?" she asked and rounded the corner to the next aisle, dumping more taffy into the top of each tube. She had a great system for self-service.

Indeed, Justice. What were we missing? I quizzed her more about the break-in at Daffy Taffy, but the visit didn't enlighten any further details. Similar time frames for each of the burglaries. Maybe it was time for extra security. If the businesses banded together, we might at least get someone for a graveyard shift. Would that be cheaper than our insurance rates going up? The problem appeared so simple, but the solution was complex. More data was needed. I squeezed my eyes shut as I exited the store, willing my brain to pop out a clue in front of me.

CHAPTER TWELVE

I leaned against the wall outside, dropping my backpack to the ground. Reaching to my back pocket, I retrieved my phone to see if Linda had texted me. Nothing. Though I expected unless the place was on fire, I wouldn't hear from her. She took care of so much. We hadn't talked yet about any schedule changes after she and Unkie married. But I was sure it would only be a matter of time before they both wanted to cut back their work hours to enjoy their adventures together. Shoving off from the wall, I lugged my backpack to my next destination, working my way to the next business along the boardwalk.

I opened the door to Checkered Past Antiques, and the smell of coffee wafted over me. A pot brewed for Unkie that invited anyone back for a chat. Sometimes I think he had the store just so he could gab with people. His personable manner worked well to impart the stories of the antique's past to his prospective customers. At times, I was sure there was a bit of embellishment for some pieces.

"Hey, Uncle Jack," I greeted. A clang arose from the corner, sounding like china dishes hitting together. I jumped, placing my hand on my chest.

"Hi, Tilly." Carlos poked his head over the stacks of antiques on the tables. He turned and pointed toward the coffee corner.

Nodding, I headed back to join Unkie. He bent forward in his chair, forearms on his knees, head bowed.

"What's wrong?" That man was never down. His exuberance spilled over to everyone in earshot of him, always bringing others up.

Slowly raising from his seat, his bones cracked. He reached out and held my upper arm and pecked me on the cheek. Standing back, he waved off his sullen demeanor. "Just an old man pity party. I'm done with it, though."

"This nonsense has to stop." I headed to the coffeepot and poured a steaming cup. This was my sanctuary here with Unkie, where we solved the world's problems.

"Jack, it's worse than we thought." Carlos approached us with a clipboard. "I've noted at least twelve of those items you listed are definitely gone."

"OK, Carlos. Thank you," Unkie said, wheeling to face me. "Before you interrogate me . . ."

I suspected he knew I had been out quizzing the business owners. There were no secrets in this town, especially from Uncle Jack. So far I had escaped any lecture from Barney, and I hoped I could continue my snooping, I mean evidence gathering, until I had something solid. I sat, notebook on my lap, ready to transcribe this latest discovery.

Without me saying a word, Uncle Jack continued, "Linda and I went on a trip to Oakwood. The pawn shop owner is a friend who called me about some good stuff he wanted me to have first crack at."

"That's not right!" Unkie's shop had been hit hard and was ripe for a burglar who could pretty easily make some quick money.

"I've got insurance. Plus, now we have more details to provide Barney with his search to arrest someone," Unkie said. "My concern is for your safety, Tilly." He sat opposite the table from me, resuming his coffee drinking.

"I'm more mad than afraid, Unkie." Glancing down at my notebook, I willed the pages to reveal a more concrete clue. Something to lead in a direction to solve this mystery.

"Fiona?"

"That situation sends me over the ledge. I am convinced the burglaries are related to the murder. She's as good as can be expected, which is not good at all."

"Hang in there, hon. I know a day at a time seems like ten, but Barney will figure this out." He knew more than anyone about patience in an investigation. Arrested in the past for a crime he didn't commit, he had to sit in jail while the police work went at its pace. He had to have been the most upbeat prisoner of all time.

"You know patience isn't my strong suit." I gave him a hug. "Love you, Unkie. I should get back to the bakery." I waved to Carlos on the way out, grateful Unkie had him to help with the shop. It was time for me to find more help at the bakery to relieve Linda. She would likely never ask for it, so I needed to make it happen for her and Unkie.

I scurried along the sidewalk on my return to the bakery, my heart hurting for Unkie's loss. Shaking my head, I attempted to replace my thoughts to the future of the bakery. Fiona and I had brainstormed so many ideas for growth, and I was ready to move forward. In my former life back east, I perennially put my goals and dreams on hold, yielding to others. I knew both Unkie and Fiona would have none of that if I paused at all on my grand plan.

One last stop. Mocha Joe's, always abuzz, was surprisingly quiet for this time of day. A barista served two customers at the counter while Joe was flitting around, I suspected preparing for the next rush.

Moving to the beverage pickup location, I said, "Joe, do you have just a sec?"

Pulling his head up as he finished filling the cup dispenser, he said, "Anything for you, Tilly. What's up?"

Over Joe's shoulder, I spotted Ronnie again. Messy head of curls, clothes and uniform a bit disheveled. If he was here again, Joe must be OK with his performance. I gasped in a quick breath and held it.

Joe followed my gaze and said, "He's actually doing well so far."

I was skeptical, but Joe was an incredibly savvy business owner. And certainly the right fit for a person could make a big difference. If it worked out, I was happy for both of them.

"On my rounds this morning, just trying to see if anyone remembered any more about the burglaries." It was worth a try, but so far my information gathering made me feel worse than when I started. Similar patterns to the time of the crime. Mostly the burglar made a mess, possibly to cover what they had taken. Maybe my thought pattern was headed the wrong direction. Was the burglary just a cover for vandalism? Did the person have a grudge against the Belle Harbor businesses for some reason? Were they turned down for a business license and trying to get back at everyone? The picture quickly became convoluted.

"I don't know what I can add. Seems similar to others. A huge mess and not a lot of stuff they could take to easily fence it for a quick buck," Joe said, raising his hand to greet one of his regulars. "Sorry, Tilly. I have to get back at it."

"Thank you," I said. A throb began behind my left eye. Emerging into the ocean air, I felt like sprinting toward the water and jumping in to wash all of this away. If only it were that easy to come out with a fresh start. Fiona might be in for a long haul. I needed to brace myself that this mystery might take one or more turns for the worse before it got better. It had to ultimately end up better. There was no other option.

CHAPTER THIRTEEN

I peered through the glass door to a crowd inside Fiona's. I hoped my now daily visits were coming across as supportive as opposed to nosy, though they were both. My shoulders slumped as I spotted Barney in the mix. This was an early appearance, and I prayed it was good news. I could hear raised voices through the door. Gulping, I shoved it open. At least I could be there for my friend.

All heads swiveled my direction and the only noise I could hear was glasses clanking in the bar. Fiona stepped toward me, dried tears on her cheeks. I grabbed her hand and returned her to the group, glaring at Barney to explain himself.

"Tilly," he started. I knew in my heart of hearts this was the last thing he wanted to do. But not only did he have to follow the law and be fair, he had to show it. Anybody else as a suspect might already have been in jail, at least given what I knew so far. Through all of my snooping, the case against Fiona only got stronger, and any other suspects drifted from suspicion.

Two people I didn't know also mingled around. "Barney. Can you just hold off a little longer?" I pleaded, holding my palms together in front of me.

"Do you know something you'd like to share?" he asked. I couldn't divulge my wild theory yet until I confirmed my assumption. Wrongly accusing someone was an act that could never be undone. Would he trust me enough to give Fiona more time?

"Well, this is all a bit too much," said the woman opposite me. From her jacket with the label of Health Department, and her name Bronwyn stitched below it, along with the clipboard in her hand down at her side, I concluded she was the replacement inspector.

I entered the middle of the group with my arm outstretched. No sense getting off on the wrong foot with her, as she would eventually visit the bakery. "I'm Tilly. Just wanted to check on my friend."

She tipped her head, staring at my hand as I continued to hold it out an awkward amount of time without shaking. "I know who you are too."

OK, then. I would give her the benefit of the doubt for now. These were highly unusual circumstances for us all. I dropped my arm to my side and stepped to her right.

We all jumped as the sound of breaking glass echoed from the bar. Stacy and a guy I didn't know looked our way in unison. "Sorry, everyone. We'll get that cleaned up," Stacy said. The guy retrieved the broom and dustpan and sheepishly bowed his head. That must be Ronnie's replacement. Not a good start to your first day. Fiona didn't need more drama in her life right now. Worrying about her employees and place of business might send her off the edge.

"As I was saying, Fiona," Bronwyn continued in a snarky tone.

She was all business. I was at a loss how to help my friend, hoping my presence at least was some comfort.

"You won't get special dispensation from me like you did from Holly," Bronwyn said.

Fiona's eyes widened. "Special?" she yelled. "You have got to be kidding me!"

Bronwyn pulled the clipboard up and flipped through several pages. "Yeah. I don't see that you ever paid a fine on these violations." Holding the clipboard toward Fiona, she said, "That preferential treatment stops now."

"Tilly, can you believe this?" Fiona paced in and out of the circle. I had never seen my friend so agitated, but who could blame her for the outburst? I only wished it hadn't been in front of Barney, adding fuel to the fire of her demeanor toward the inspectors.

Supporting my friend with her reasonable supposition, I entered the fray. "Maybe there's a mistake. Fiona's violations were all appealed and found without merit." My face warmed, and I hoped I didn't just do myself in as a target.

"Nobody in our office believed it. You had Ronnie working here, right?" Bronwyn asked.

Dropping her voice a couple of octaves, Fiona said, "Yes. What does that have to do with anything?"

Barney continued to watch this volley of accusations. Glancing at him, I tried to get a read on his position. Was this hurting Fiona's case? Making eye contact with me, he gave the slightest shake of his head. What did that mean? Was he signaling that he was resigned to arrest Fiona? Her anger might have been the final straw for Barney to believe she might have killed Holly, even if it wasn't intentional.

"Holly always let you off the hook because her nephew worked here," Bronwyn said.

Fiona stumbled back a few steps and looked at Barney and me, angrily shaking her head. I couldn't tell if she genuinely didn't know that or she was upset that she was outed and possibly implicated in Holly's death. Either way, she was still my best friend.

"That's ridiculous," I said, sure that I had just sealed my fate with future inspections.

"Is it?" Bronwyn asked. She had a point, and that would explain all the violations that were vacated. Maybe Holly was writing Fiona up to cover for the special treatment so that nobody got suspicious? But the sixty-four-thousand-dollar question: Was Fiona in on it? And if so, why?

"Fiona," Barney uttered.

She whimpered, appearing to conclude the next step.

I quickly moved to face Fiona and grabbed her hands as her head drooped. "We'll figure this out. I promise." I stepped back as I heard the clinking metal of the handcuffs. My pulse raced as I pondered whether I made a guarantee I couldn't keep. If Fiona could just wait a smidge longer. I hung my hope on my far-fetched theory that I had to test.

"I'm sorry, Fiona." Barney continued reading her Miranda rights as she turned around and held her arms behind her back. In my wildest dreams, I never could have envisioned this scene. My desperate, last-ditch attempt to solve this just had to work.

"Tilly," Fiona uttered.

"We've got this," I said, every muscle in my body tensed for battle.

Barney silently led the sobbing Fiona from the bar. You could hear a pin drop. Bronwyn's eyes were as big as saucers. "Wow," she said. Yeah, wow. What did you expect when you threw her under the bus right in front of the police chief? I had to transition to damage control mode right now, even though I wanted to throttle Bronwyn. No sense in two arrests.

"Look," I pleaded with Bronwyn. "Could you please extend a little grace and at least come back tomorrow?" That would give me a moment to gain some composure and hopefully make sure Stacy could take the reins of the bar for the foreseeable future.

Tucking her clipboard into the briefcase on the nearby table, she relented. OK. Immediate disaster averted. If I could ensure Stacy and crew could handle the opening today, I would have a brief opportunity to validate my assumption, with a plan to return to the bar around dinner to check on things. Could I pull this off by the end of the day to give Fiona some good news?

Bronwyn left without another word as I huddled with Stacy to make a game plan. As distressed as we all were, Stacy had mustered her game face to take over. With only one other mission on my mind, I exited the bar, crossing my fingers on both hands.

CHAPTER FOURTEEN

Backing up against the wall outside Mocha Joe's, I closed my eyes. What would I say to Joe to convince him of my hypothesis? Did I have enough credibility with him to gain the benefit of the doubt? If this all went south, no question my lucrative business relationship with Joe would suffer. It was a chance I had to take for my friend. My instincts propelled me forward, and I was certain there was something to discover.

Pulling out my phone, I concluded there was no going back and typed out my message. I followed customers into the store and wove my way past them to reach the front counter. Joe and team were in high gear, operating like a well-oiled machine. I hated to interrupt, but my friend's life depended on it. And I knew in my heart she would do the same for me. I shifted my shoulders back and stood tall, signaling Joe from the end of the counter.

He acknowledged me with a head bob, finished what he was doing, and approached. "Tilly, we're really slammed. What can I do for you?" Joe's head rotated to the large group of customers entering the store. His mouth smiled, but his eyes pleaded for me to quickly explain my request.

"Joe, you know I wouldn't ask if it wasn't critical," I started, hoping that would buy me a minute. He turned, holding his hand to the side of his mouth, "Mae, front counter," summoning reinforcements to serve the growing throng of caffeine seekers.

"OK, Tilly. You have my attention."

All might be for naught. Ronnie was nowhere in sight. Had he ghosted Joe finally, the same as he had Fiona? "This might sound like the wildest idea ever. But if you can hear me out." I offered my theory to Joe, expecting to be dismissed. My evidence was sketchy, but plausible to explain the crime spree. Joe looked down at his shirt with the Mocha Joe's Coffee Shop logo, fingering the collar.

"I didn't even notice that. I was just thrilled that he kept showing up, hoping I had gotten through to him about responsibility," Joe said. Staring at me, he continued, "I eased up on this messy dress code for a bit while he was getting up to speed."

Why would he notice the frosting? It was subtle enough to blend into Ronnie's shirt, but obvious enough to me since I work with it every day. "Don't blame yourself. He fooled all of us. When does his shift start?" I glanced at the door as more customers streamed in.

"Oh, he's here. Just in the back." Joe thumbed his hand in the direction of the storage room.

"Can we both go see him?" I must have been out of my mind confronting a criminal. Maybe being outnumbered might subdue him. Would he deny the allegations?

Joe scanned the lobby, choosing to leave the customers to his team as he lifted the counter for me to enter and follow him.

I needed to gather my thoughts to decide how to approach this for maximum results. I was in lockstep with Joe as he turned into the stockroom.

Ronnie lifted his head. "Hi boss," he jovially greeted, seemingly unaware of the ton of bricks about to come down on him. Standing as he realized Joe wasn't alone, he looked back and forth between us, his brows puckered. "What's going on? Is Fiona OK?"

Well, no. She's not. Quite interesting that would be his first comment upon seeing me.

Joe turned and stepped aside, allowing me to fully enter the room.

I gulped, throwing all caution to the wind and sliding my feet forward. "We have a question for you," I started, glancing at Joe to loop him into my strategy. How could I present the information neutrally to get Ronnie to talk?

He set the sleeve of coffee cups on a nearby box and said, "OK. Anything to help Fiona."

His focus on her was heartwarming, except for the fact he left her to take the blame for murdering Holly. "Ronnie, I know you are responsible for the burglaries at the businesses." Maybe starting with the least of his crimes and building up could at least get him talking.

"No way. I would never do that," he pleaded, voice raised an octave as he gazed toward Joe.

Softening my tone to de-escalate, I said, "I saw your shirt the other day with the same frosting on the collar as I have on my cupcakes. On the day someone burglarized the bakery."

That little tidbit would be hard for him to explain. I waited as he turned sideways, looking away. Joe cleared his throat, prompting Ronnie to return his attention to me. Silence continued.

Unless he confessed, my theory would be out the window. I could easily paint a picture of where Ronnie was prime suspect. The only piece missing was motive. Why would he burglarize and subsequently kill Holly, who I now knew was his aunt?

Lifting his apron over his head and tossing it to the ground, he passed by me and met Joe, who blocked the door. This was not going according to plan. All that Ronnie had to do was say we were holding him hostage, and we would be in trouble.

"Why would you hurt Fiona that way?" I desperately went to the heart for my last attempt at a confession.

Ronnie stopped in his tracks and hung his head. "It wasn't my idea," he muttered.

"Whose idea was it?" I maintained a soft tone.

Silence. The only sound from the bustling customers in the lobby.

"Did Holly put you up to it?" Joe asked.

Ronnie plopped into a chair along the wall, burying his head in his hands. "We didn't want to hurt anyone," he mumbled toward the floor.

Joe and I exchanged a glance.

"But it went too far at Fiona's," I said. "What happened, Ronnie?" My voice was almost a whisper.

He stood so quickly the chair scooted out from under him and slid into the box of cups, knocking all of them onto the floor. "I didn't mean it. Holly said the businesses would be fine. They had insurance." Attempting to exit the room, Ronnie ran directly into Barney in the doorway.

That man made it just in the nick of time. If Ronnie had escaped, I wasn't sure we would ever see him again.

"Barney?" I said.

"I got all of that, Tilly," he replied, spinning Ronnie around and slapping cuffs on his wrists. Reading Ronnie his rights, he arrested him for the burglaries and the murder of Holly Pickett.

Squeezing my eyes shut, I really hoped this drama at Joe's didn't hurt his business. "Can I-"

"As soon as I get back to the station, I'll release Fiona," Barney said, escorting Ronnie away.

My friend would be free. I knew it would take some time to recover from the ordeal, and I would help her any way I could. My muscles relaxed, almost to the point of collapsing onto the floor, as Barney escorted Ronnie away.

"Tilly, that was really brave of you," Joe said.

I sniffled, grabbing a nearby napkin to wipe my tears and nose. "I think it was more a combo of anger and stubbornness that they wrongly accused Fiona."

"She's very lucky to have you as a friend. And we are all grateful to have you in Belle Harbor." Joe wrapped me in a hug as I let loose blubbering, finally able to release my pent-up stress.

CHAPTER FIFTEEN

Uncle Jack and Linda faced each other, hands intertwined. Unkie had a warmth on his face I had never seen. The officiant finished, and the newly married couple leaned in to kiss just as tiny snowflakes drifted down. Linda straightened, tears in her eyes as the dream wedding came to life. As Jack and Linda were introduced as Mr. and Mrs., Barney stepped forward with a jacket for the bride. It was the right decision to use the deck for the ceremony. The snow-capped mountains in front of us all served as a stunning backdrop. The space heaters throughout kept us warm enough until we could escape inside near the roaring fire in the massive river rock fireplace.

As Unkie and Linda returned down the aisle to head inside, I saw Justin wink at me. No doubt the event had further sparked his interest in marriage. Was I ready for that? We had only been going out for a relatively short time, but I was certain I could see myself with him for the rest of my life. I shivered. Linda's maid of honor and I began our trek to warmer temperatures as I spotted Barney and Florence holding hands, gazing into each other's eyes. Maybe they would be the next to marry?

White lights twinkled along the perimeter of the great room of the lodge as the guests returned from the deck. Music played in the background, and they prepared food on the buffet table.

The newlyweds huddled near the fireplace. The crowd moved toward them for congratulations. This event ranked in my top five for the happiest time of my life. The pure joy of the moment would stay with me for quite some time. For all the recent drama, the ceremony came together nicely, albeit not without last-minute rushing around.

I approached Fiona, seated in a side chair apart from the fireplace and the center of attention. Her stare was in the distance, far beyond the immediate scene. Sitting on the arm of the chair, I reached for her hand. She tipped her head up, and no amount of makeup could cover the dark circles under her eyes. It had been a few days since they had released her from jail, but the damage done would take some time to fade.

"Tilly," Fiona choked the word out.

"I know," I replied, squeezing her hand.

"Just need a minute to regroup." If it were me, I would need way more than that. "Thank you, Tilly. I don't know how you put all of it together, but I'm forever grateful."

There wasn't anything I wouldn't do for my friend. She didn't deserve any of that and got snared in Holly and Ronnie's scheme.

Justin sidled next to me and draped his arm around my shoulder, and I leaned my head toward him. No matter how crazy or dramatic my life got, he was there for me.

"Good to see you, Fiona." Barney joined our little group.

"With no bars between us." Fiona chuckled and stood, embracing Barney. A flicker of humor was a good sign of healing progress.

"I owe some thanks to this one, and Joe." Barney poked his thumb in my direction.

I shrugged. Somehow I couldn't help myself. Once my brain spotted a puzzle to solve, it wouldn't quit until there were answers that made sense. And if I could help my friend, all the better.

"I just feel bad for Ronnie. I don't think he meant to do it. He just got caught up, and it spun out of control," Fiona said. Her heart for her former employee was admirable. Not sure I would have the same grace for someone, especially if they let me take the blame for murder. Was this just a case of a good person who made an awful choice? Was there such a thing?

"Yeah, he sang like a birdie on the way to jail," Barney shared. "I think partly to save his own skin."

Dishes clanged from the other side of the room, signaling final touches on the buffet table. Snow had begun to fall more heavily, making the scene appear as if we were in a snow globe.

"I just wish people who needed help would ask for it instead of resorting to crime to solve their problems. Maybe if I would have known more about Ronnie, I could have done something," Fiona said, shaking her head.

"Fiona, none of this is your fault," Barney said. "Ronnie had pressures from his mom at home, who threatened to kick him out if he didn't pay his fair share. Somehow, Holly convinced him to steal, to make money for himself and cover her gambling debts. And once he started, there was no turning back. It sounds like there was a confrontation at Fiona's and he grabbed the nearest thing he could find. More to scare Holly. Who knew frozen ravioli, used just right, could kill someone?"

"Enough shop talk," Unkie said and neared Fiona for a hug. Scanning our little circle, he continued, "What a perfect place for a wedding, huh?" His gaze stopped at Justin.

My face warmed, and not from the nearby roaring fire. Planning Unkie and Linda's wedding had given me many ideas for my own. I most definitely wanted to be married, and I assumed given current circumstance, it would be to Justin. Nothing in life was guaranteed. Was I ready? He had jokingly mimed a proposal a few times and teased, but I knew as soon as I gave the green light, it would be for real. What was I waiting for?

"So about those books?" I diverted to a safer topic. Justin and I would take over running Checkered Past Antiques while Unkie and Linda were on their honeymoon. Thankfully, we also had Carlos to fill in when we couldn't be there. A collection of rare books had been promised to Uncle Jack. His contacts in the antique business reached far and wide. And his people personality had cultivated many long-lasting, trusting relationships in the business. He had become the regional go to for people to pass along their treasures to others for enjoyment.

"Carlos can give you the details," Uncle Jack said. "I trust you guys."

"We better not hear anything from you on your honeymoon about business. Only pictures of the fun you're having," I said, pointing my finger at him, grinning from ear to ear. I wondered if this was a glimpse of my future. Uncle Jack cutting back on the work hours and me stepping in to do more? He had nobody else to pass along the business to. My hands were more than full with my bakery, but was there a way to do both?

The sound of silverware clinking against a glass prompted everyone's attention to the source of the noise. Servers circled the room, handing out champagne for a toast. Unkie returned to Linda's side, both of their eyes sparkling as much as the bubbly. When everyone had a glass, Barney led us in a touching toast to the newlyweds. I fully expected some good-natured ribbing between those two long-time friends, but the words couldn't have been more heartfelt. The love in the room enveloped us all as we raised our glasses.

What's Next? Cotton Candy and Chaos

With her uncle's wedding in the books, Tilly agrees to look over the antique shop while he is on his honeymoon. A set of rare books has arrived to be brokered to a local collector.

Tilly opens up when she discovers the books are missing, and the neighboring bookstore owner hints that she has rescued the books from an untimely demise.

The investigation is quickly gummed up when suspicion lands on the newcomer cotton candy vendor in town.

Can Tilly turn the page and recover the literary collection before the honeymoon is cut short in Cotton Candy and Chaos? Find out in book 12 in the Belle Harbor Cozy Mystery series.

ABOUT THE AUTHOR

Sue Hollowell is a wife and empty nester with a lot of mom left over. Finding a lot of time on her hands, and as a lover of mystery novels, she began telling the story of a character who appeared in her head. And she hasn't looked back. She likes cake, and the more frosting the better!